D0498288

A Note to Parents and Caregivers:

Read-it! Readers are for children who are just starting on the amazing road to reading. These beautiful books support both the acquisition of reading skills and the love of books.

The PURPLE LEVEL presents basic topics and objects using high frequency words and simple language patterns.

The RED LEVEL presents familiar topics using common words and repeating sentence patterns.

The BLUE LEVEL presents new ideas using a larger vocabulary and varied sentence structure.

The YELLOW LEVEL presents more challenging ideas, a broad vocabulary, and wide variety in sentence structure.

The GREEN LEVEL presents more complex ideas, an extended vocabulary range, and expanded language structures.

The ORANGE LEVEL presents a wide range of ideas and concepts using challenging vocabulary and complex language structures.

When sharing a book with your child, read in short stretches, pausing often to talk about the pictures. Have your child turn the pages and point to the pictures and familiar words. And be sure to reread favorite stories or parts of stories.

There is no right or wrong way to share books with children. Find time to read with your child, and pass on the legacy of literacy.

Adria F. Klein, Ph.D.
Professor Emeritus
California State University
San Bernardino, California

Editor: Jacqueline A. Wolfe
Page Production: Amy Bailey Muehlenhardt
Creative Director: Keith Griffin
Editorial Director: Carol Jones
Managing Editor: Catherine Neitge
The illustrations in this book were created with watercolor and colored pencil.

Picture Window Books
5115 Excelsior Boulevard
Suite 232
Minneapolis, MN 55416
877-845-8392
www.picturewindowbooks.com

Printed in the United States of America.

Library of Congress Cataloging-in-Publication Data
Klein, Adria F.
Max goes to the library / by Adria F. Klein ; illustrated by Mernie Gallagher-Cole.
p. cm. — (Read-it! readers)
Summary: Max, who loves to read, discovers all the services available to him during
a visit to the library.
ISBN 1-4048-1182-6 (hardcover)
[1. Libraries—Fiction. 2. Books and reading—Fiction. 3. Hispanic
Americans—Fiction.] I. Gallagher-Cole, Mernie, ill. II. Title. III. Series.

PZ7.K678324Max 2005
[E]—dc22   2005003854

Max
Goes to the Library

by Adria F. Klein
illustrated by Mernie Gallagher-Cole

Special thanks to our advisers for their expertise:

Adria F. Klein, Ph.D.
Professor Emeritus, California State University
San Bernardino, California

Susan Kesselring, M.A.
Literacy Educator
Rosemount-Apple Valley-Eagan (Minnesota) School District

PICTURE WINDOW BOOKS
Minneapolis, Minnesota

Max likes to read books.

Max goes to the library.

He meets the librarian.

The librarian gives him a
library card.

The librarian shows him the
children's books.

11

Max picks a book about animals.

12

13

He sits at the table and reads
his book.

A-C

→

Picture books

D-F

BOOKS

Animals

mats

Max uses a computer to find more animal books.

Max checks out three books.

Max wants to come back to the library very soon.

Max likes to read books.

23

More *Read-it!* Readers

Bright pictures and fun stories help you practice your reading skills. Look for more books at your level.

A Year of Fun by Susan Blackaby

Ann Plants a Garden by Susan Blackaby

Bess and Tess by Susan Blackaby

Dan Gets Set by Susan Blackaby

Fishing Trip by Susan Blackaby

Max Goes on the Bus by Adria F. Klein

Max Goes Shopping by Adria F. Klein

Max Goes to School by Adria F. Klein

Max Goes to the Barber by Adria F. Klein

Max Goes to the Dentist by Adria F. Klein

The Best Soccer Player by Susan Blackaby

Wes Gets a Pet by Susan Blackaby

Winter Fun for Kat by Susan Blackaby

Looking for a specific title or level? A complete list of *Read-it!* Readers is available on our Web site:
www.picturewindowbooks.com